D1489362

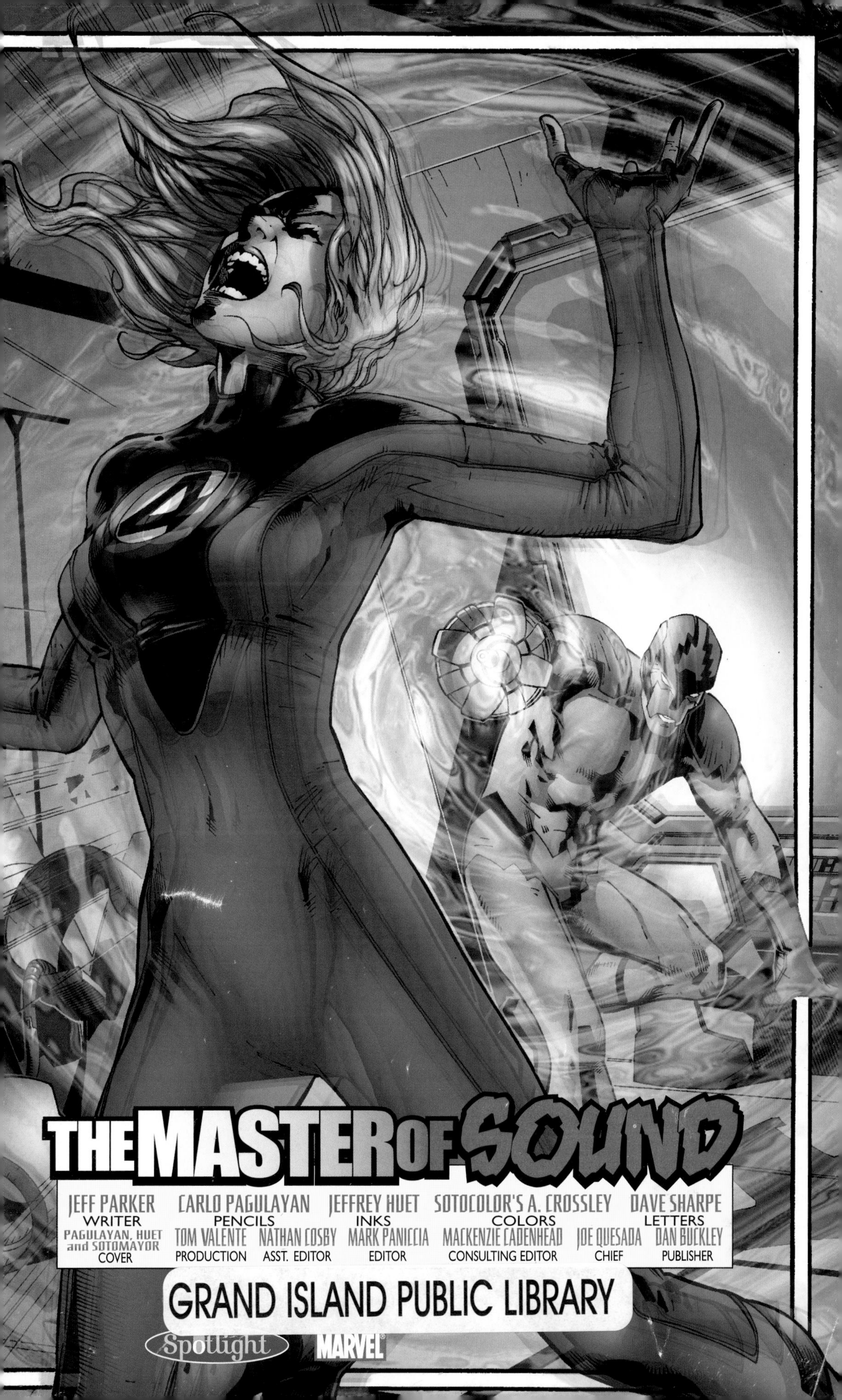
THE MASTER OF SOUND
JEFF PARKER WRITER
CARLO PAGULAYAN PENCILS
JEFFREY HUET INKS
SOTOCOLOR'S A. CROSSLEY COLORS
DAVE SHARPE LETTERS
PAGULAYAN, HUET and SOTOMAYOR COVER
TOM VALENTE PRODUCTION
NATHAN COSBY ASST. EDITOR
MARK PANICCIA EDITOR
MACKENZIE CADENHEAD CONSULTING EDITOR
JOE QUESADA CHIEF
DAN BUCKLEY PUBLISHER
Spotlight
MARVEL

VISIT US AT
www.abdopublishing.com

Reinforced library bound edition published in 2008 by Spotlight, a division of the ABDO Publishing Group, 8000 West 78th Street, Edina, Minnesota 55439. Spotlight produces high-quality reinforced library bound editions for schools and libraries. Published by agreement with Marvel Characters, Inc

Library of Congress Cataloging-in-Publication Data

Parker, Jeff, 1966-
   The master of sound / Jeff Parker, writer ; Carlo Pagulayan, pencils ; Jeffrey Huet, inks ; A. Crossley, colors ; Dave Sharpe, letters ; Pagulayan, Huet and Sotomayor, cover. -- Reinforced library bound ed.
      p. cm. -- (Fantastic Four)
   "Marvel age"--Cover.
   Revision of issue 9 of Marvel adventures Fantastic Four.
   ISBN 978-1-59961-391-8
   1. Graphic novels. I. Pagulayan, Carlo. II. Marvel adventures Fantastic Four. 9. III. Title.

PN6728.F33P37 2008
741.5'973--dc22

2007020241

All Spotlight books have reinforced library bindings and are manufactured in the United States of America.

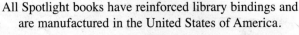

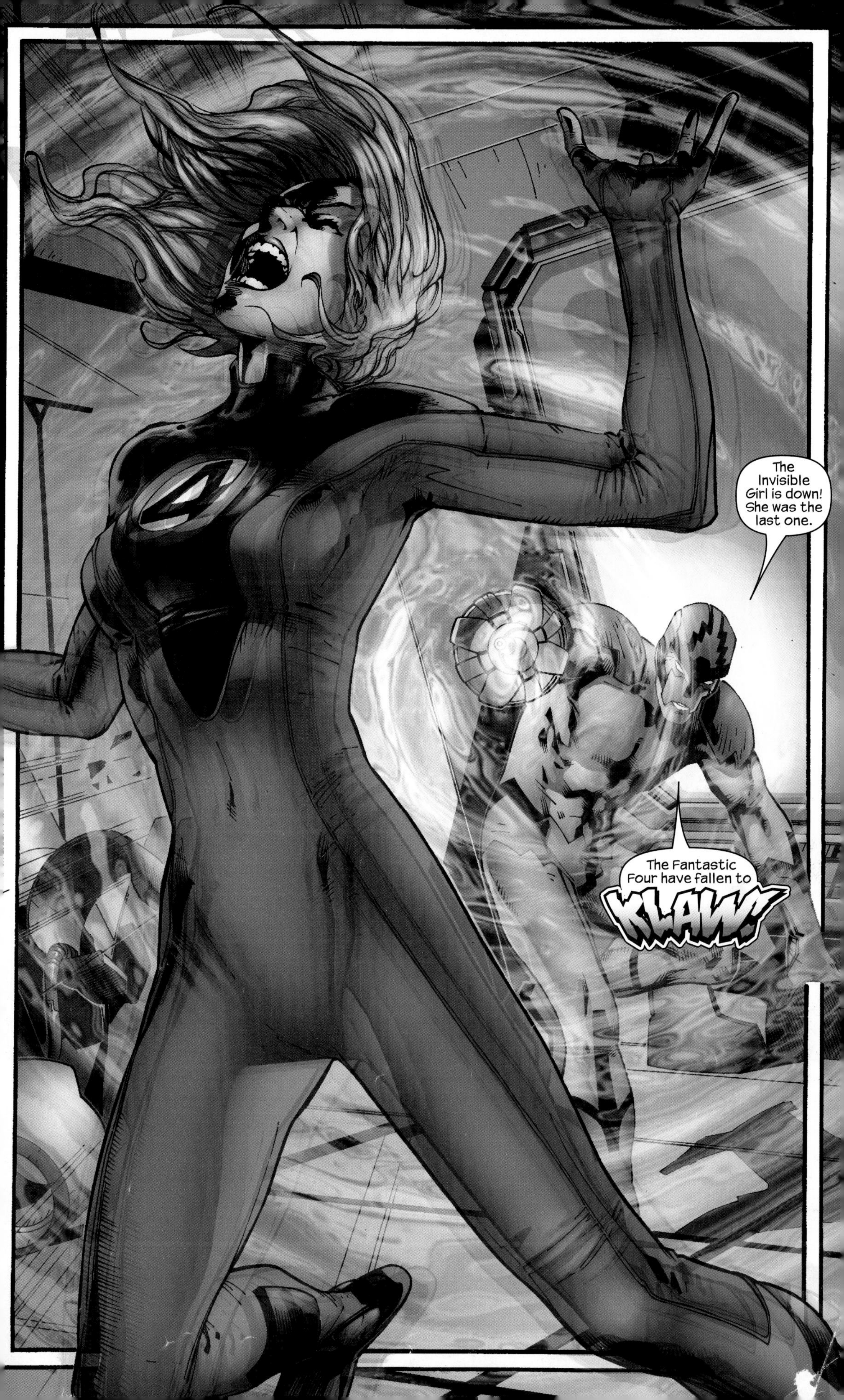
The Invisible Girl is down! She was the last one.
The Fantastic Four have fallen to
KLAW!

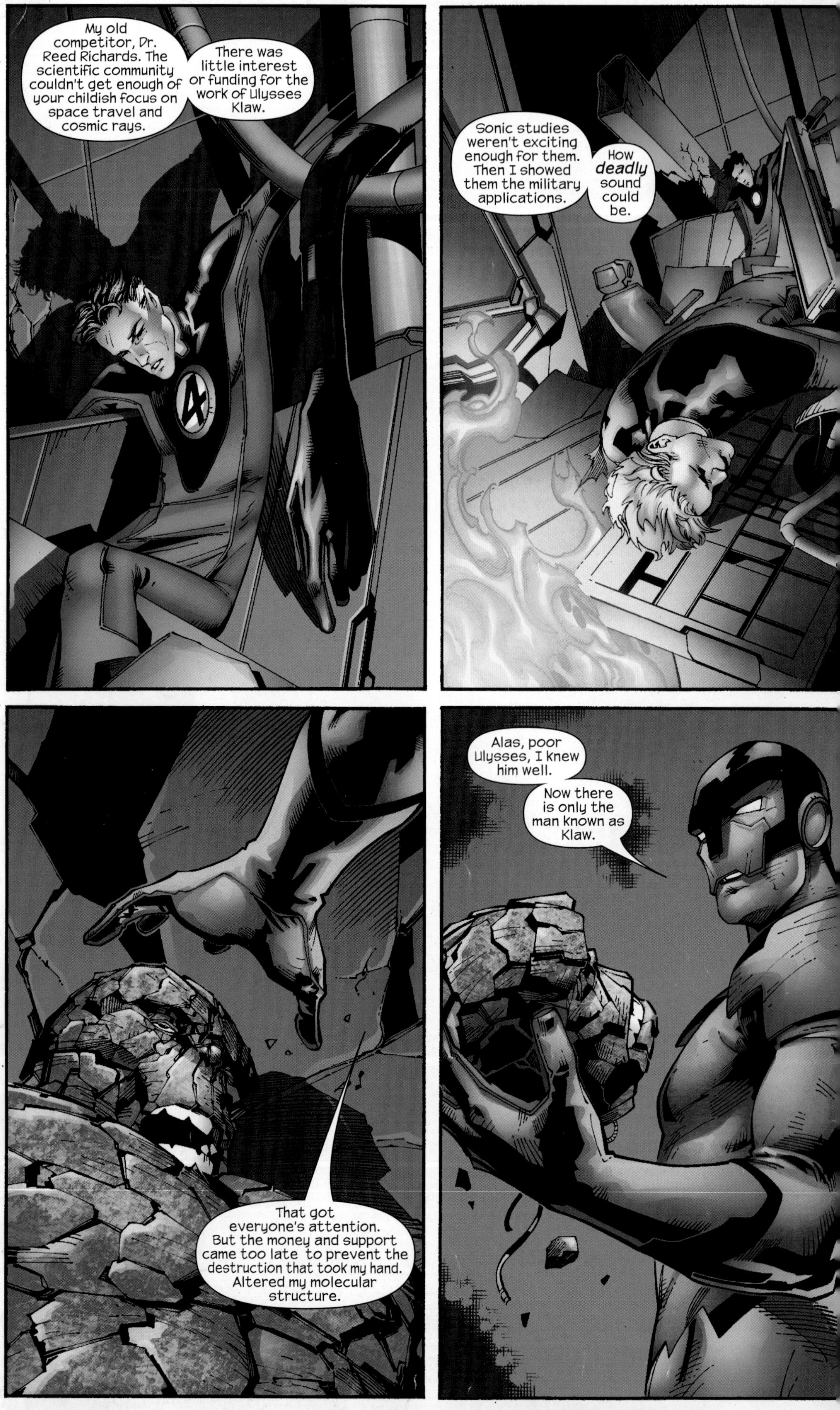

My old competitor, Dr. Reed Richards. The scientific community couldn't get enough of your childish focus on space travel and cosmic rays.
There was little interest or funding for the work of Ulysses Klaw.
Sonic studies weren't exciting enough for them. Then I showed them the military applications.
How *deadly* sound could be.
That got everyone's attention. But the money and support came too late to prevent the destruction that took my hand. Altered my molecular structure.
Alas, poor Ulysses, I knew him well.
Now there is only the man known as Klaw.

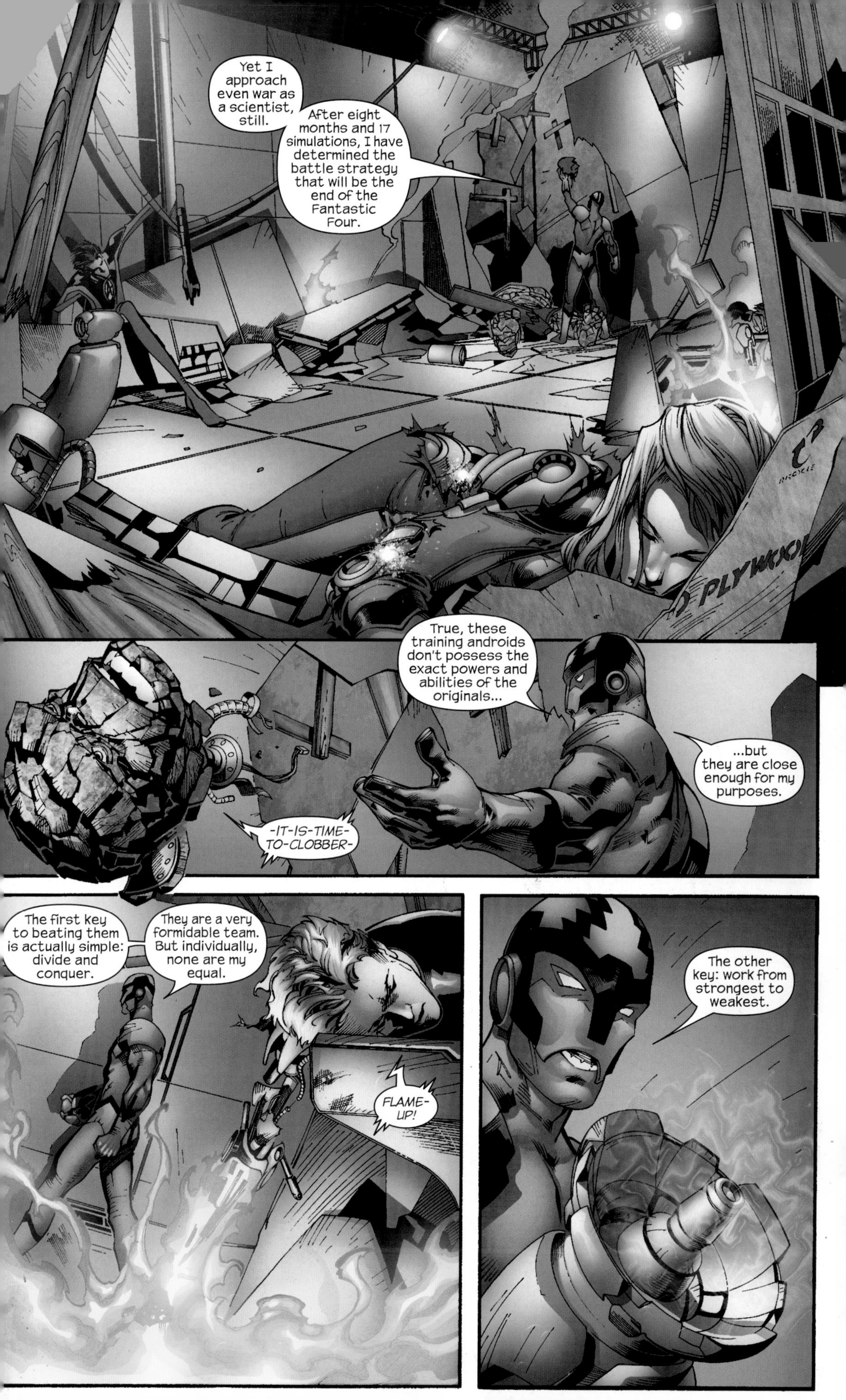
Yet I approach even war as a scientist, still.
After eight months and 17 simulations, I have determined the battle strategy that will be the end of the Fantastic Four.
PLYWOO
True, these training androids don't possess the exact powers and abilities of the originals...
...but they are close enough for my purposes.
-IT-IS-TIME-TO-CLOBBER-
The first key to beating them is actually simple: divide and conquer.
They are a very formidable team. But individually, none are my equal.
FLAME-UP!
The other key: work from strongest to weakest.

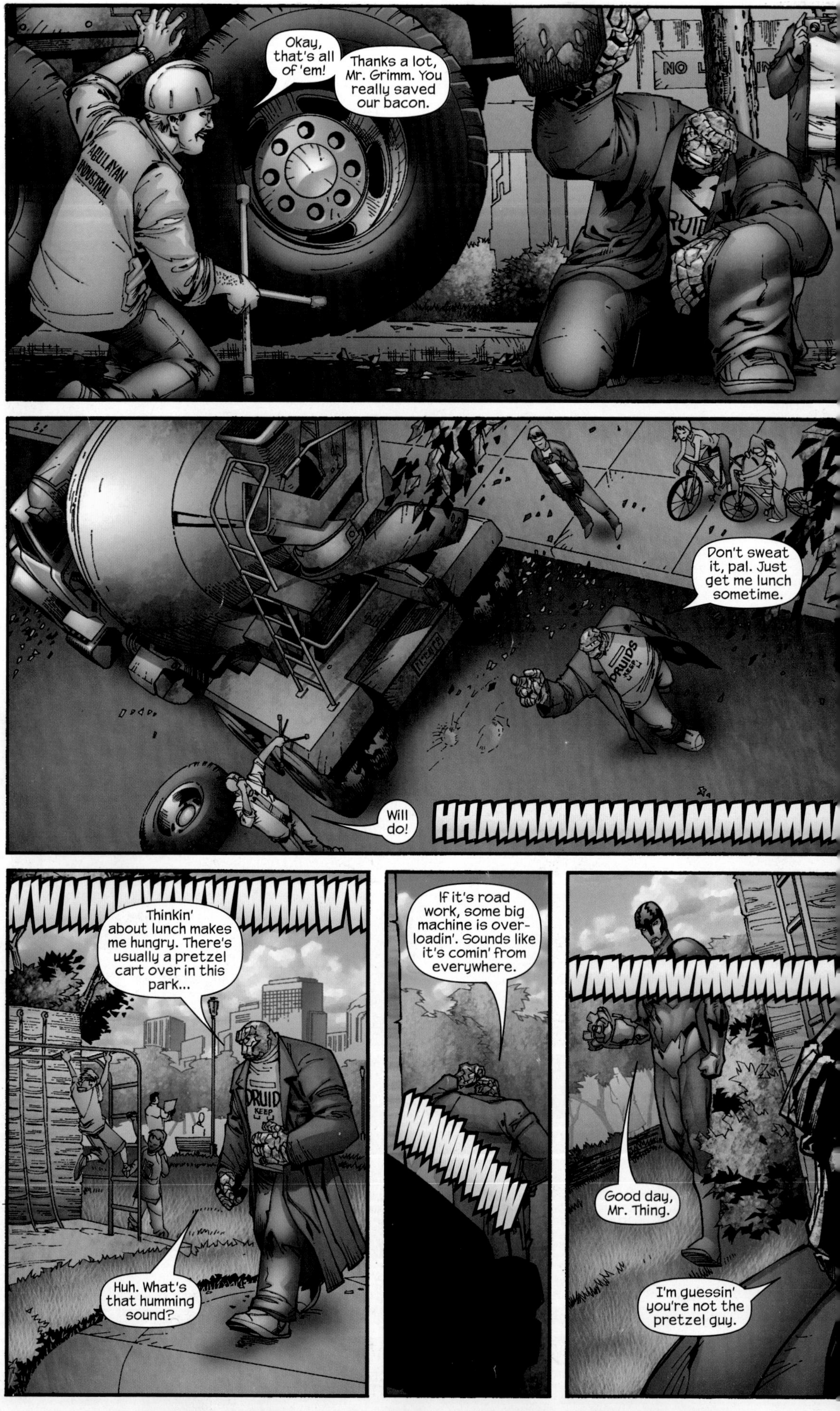
Okay, that's all of 'em!
Thanks a lot, Mr. Grimm. You really saved our bacon.
Don't sweat it, pal. Just get me lunch sometime.
Will do!
HHMMMMMMMMMMMMM
WMMMWWWMMMWW
Thinkin' about lunch makes me hungry. There's usually a pretzel cart over in this park...
Huh. What's that humming sound?
If it's road work, some big machine is over-loadin'. Sounds like it's comin' from everywhere.
WMWMWM
VMWMWMWMWM
Good day, Mr. Thing.
I'm guessin' you're not the pretzel guy.

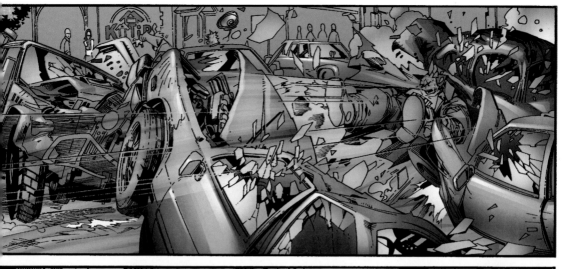

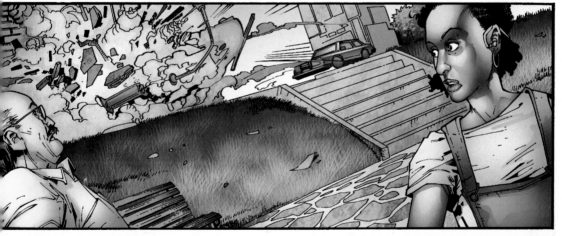

ESTABLISHMENT
CONDEMNED
CITY ENGR OFC
MANHATTAN

OFF
LIMITS
ANG LAMOK

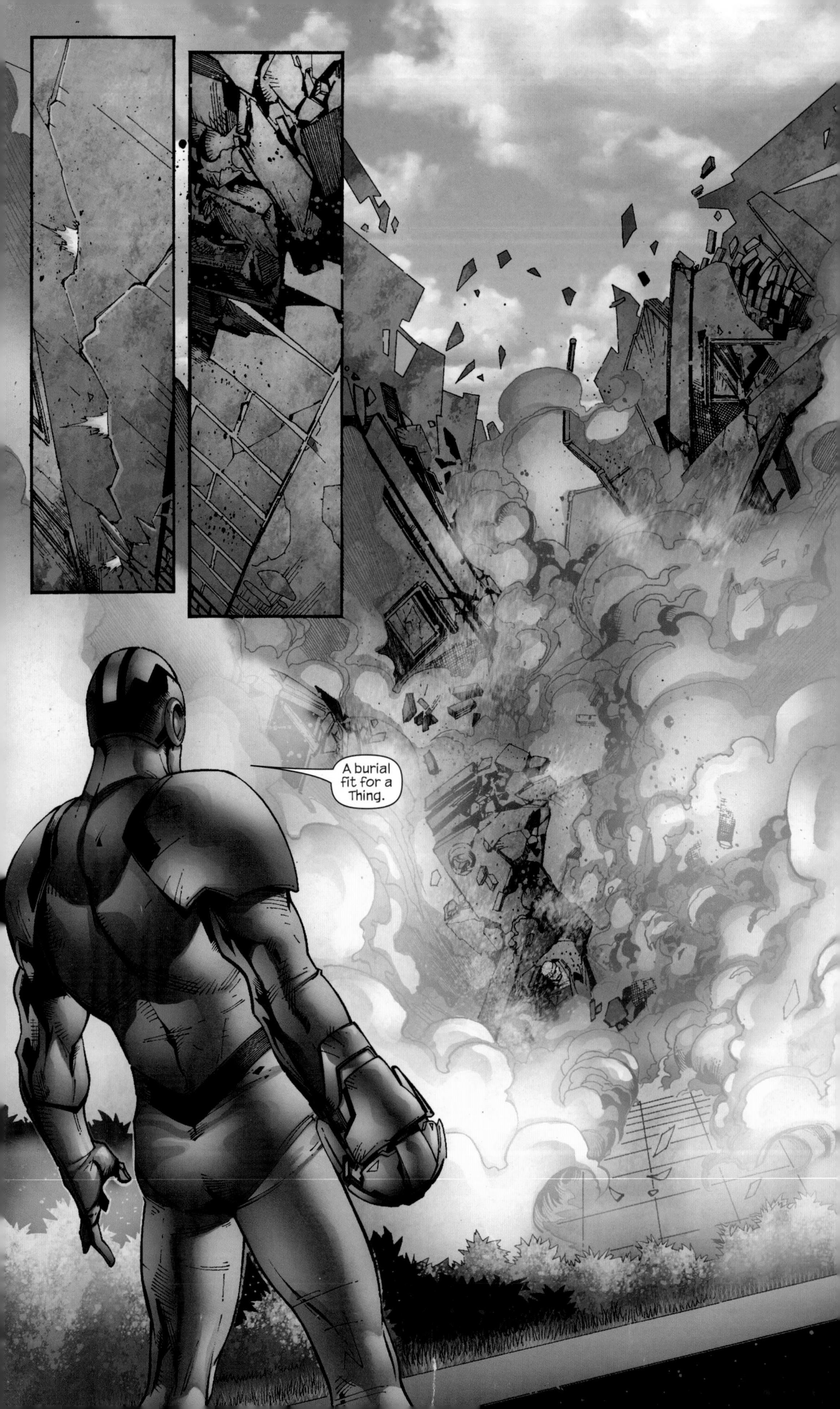
A burial fit for a Thing.

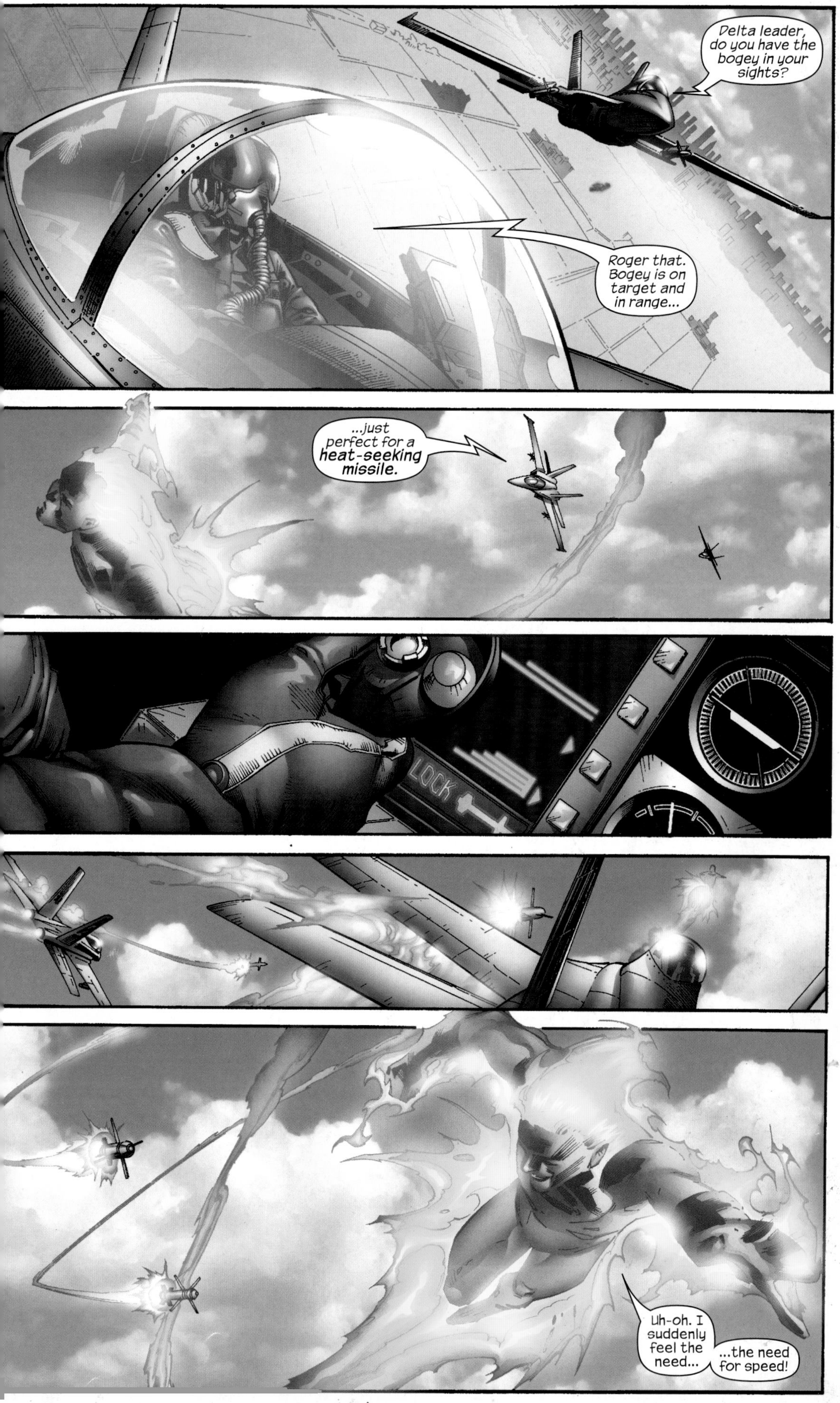

Delta leader, do you have the bogey in your sights?
Roger that. Bogey is on target and in range...
...just perfect for a heat-seeking missile.
LOCK
Uh-oh. I suddenly feel the need...
...the need for speed!

Hoo-Whee! These things don't want to be ditched!

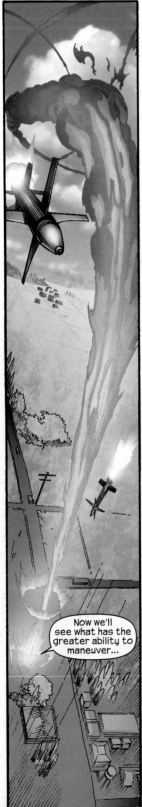

Now we'll see what has the greater ability to maneuver...

The AIM-9 Sidewinder missile...

...or The Human Torch!

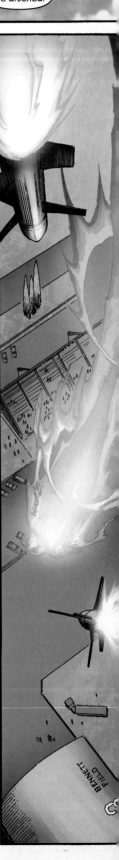

BENNETT FIELD

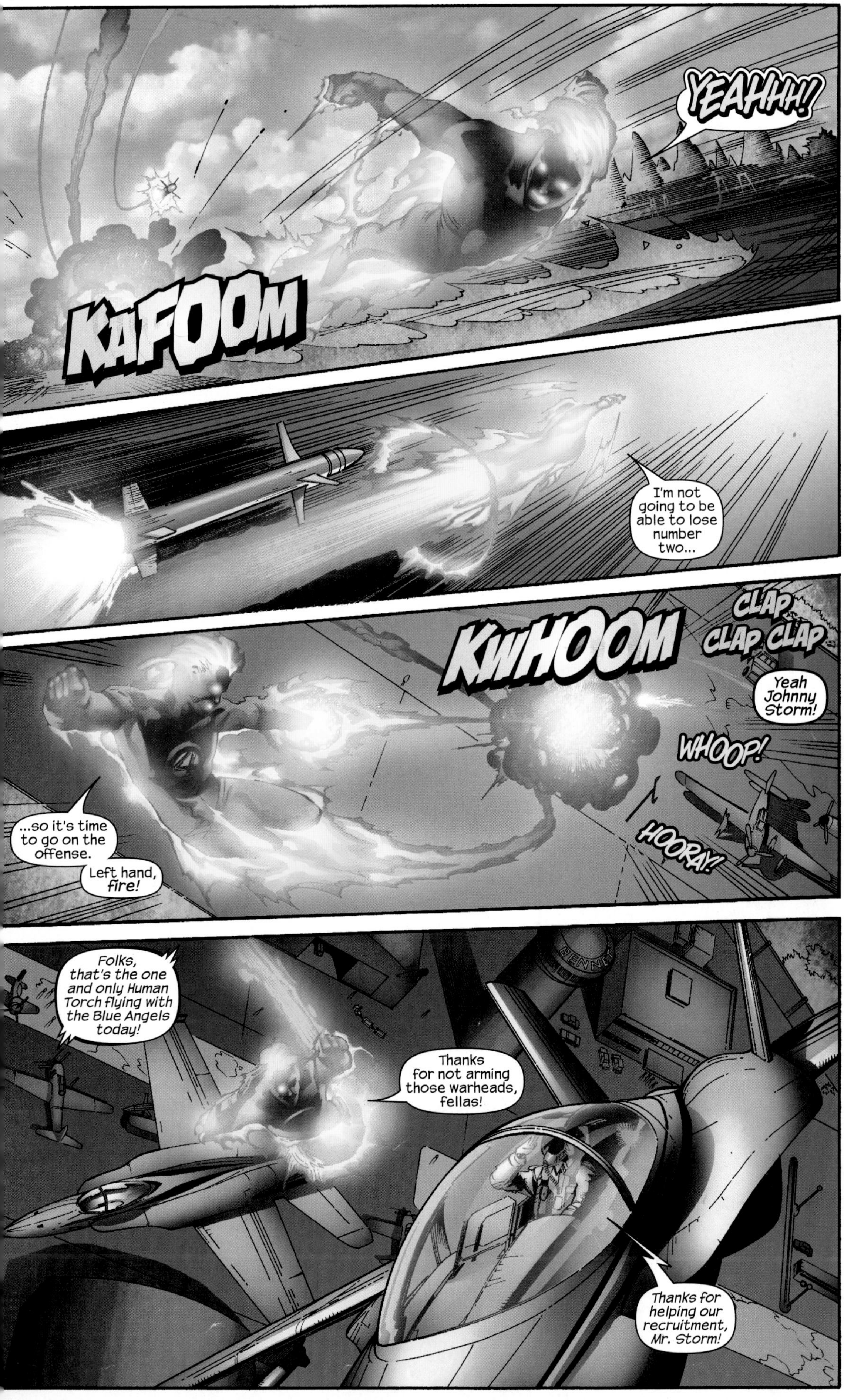
YEAHHH!
KAFOOM
I'm not going to be able to lose number two...
KWHOOM
CLAP CLAP CLAP
Yeah Johnny Storm!
WHOOP!
HOORAY!
...so it's time to go on the offense.
Left hand, fire!
Folks, that's the one and only Human Torch flying with the Blue Angels today!
Thanks for not arming those warheads, fellas!
Thanks for helping our recruitment, Mr. Storm!

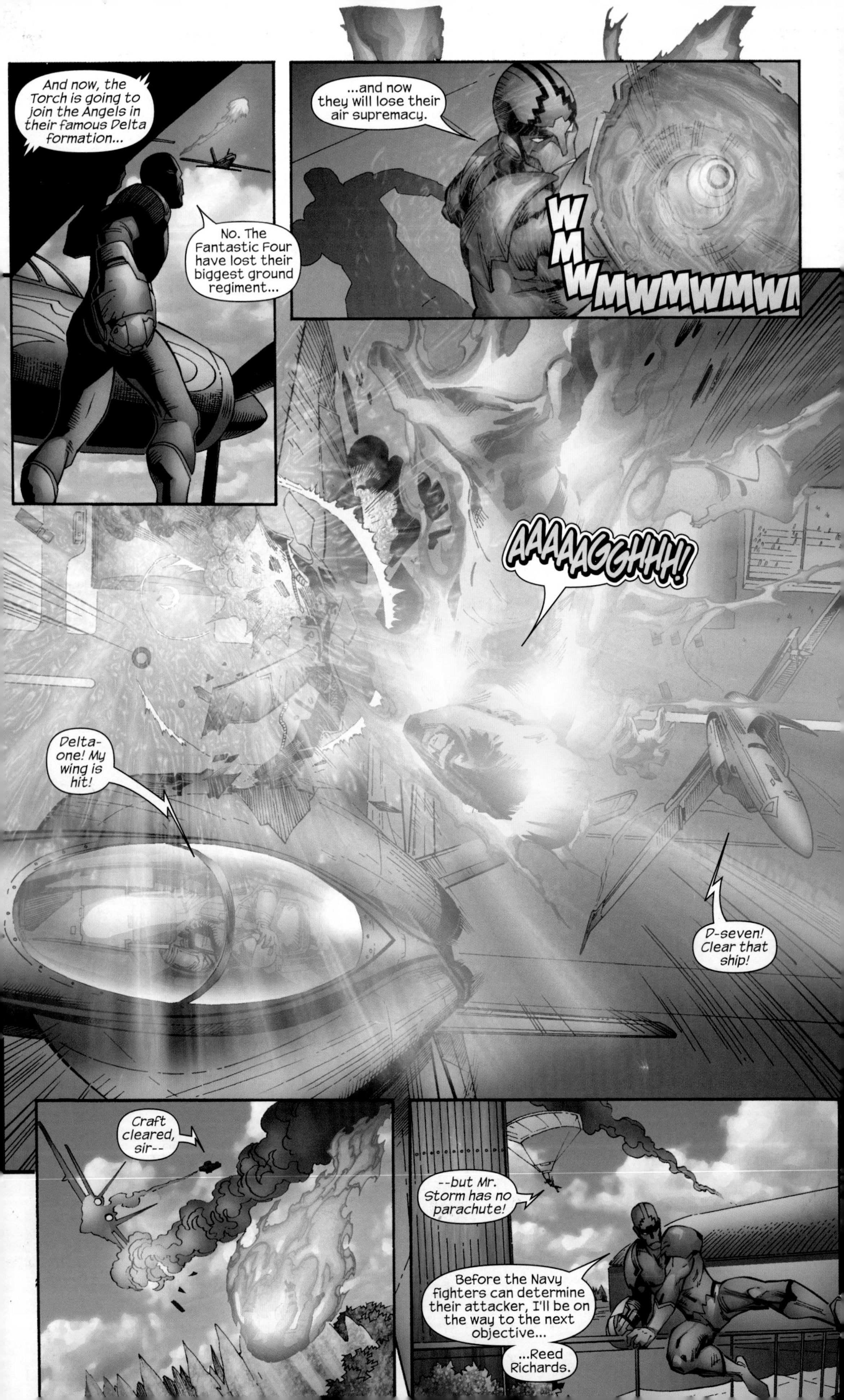
And now, the Torch is going to join the Angels in their famous Delta formation...
No. The Fantastic Four have lost their biggest ground regiment...
...and now they will lose their air supremacy.
WMWMWMWMWMWM
AAAAAGGHHH!
Delta-one! My wing is hit!
D-seven! Clear that ship!
Craft cleared, sir--
--but Mr. Storm has no parachute!
Before the Navy fighters can determine their attacker, I'll be on the way to the next objective...
...Reed Richards.

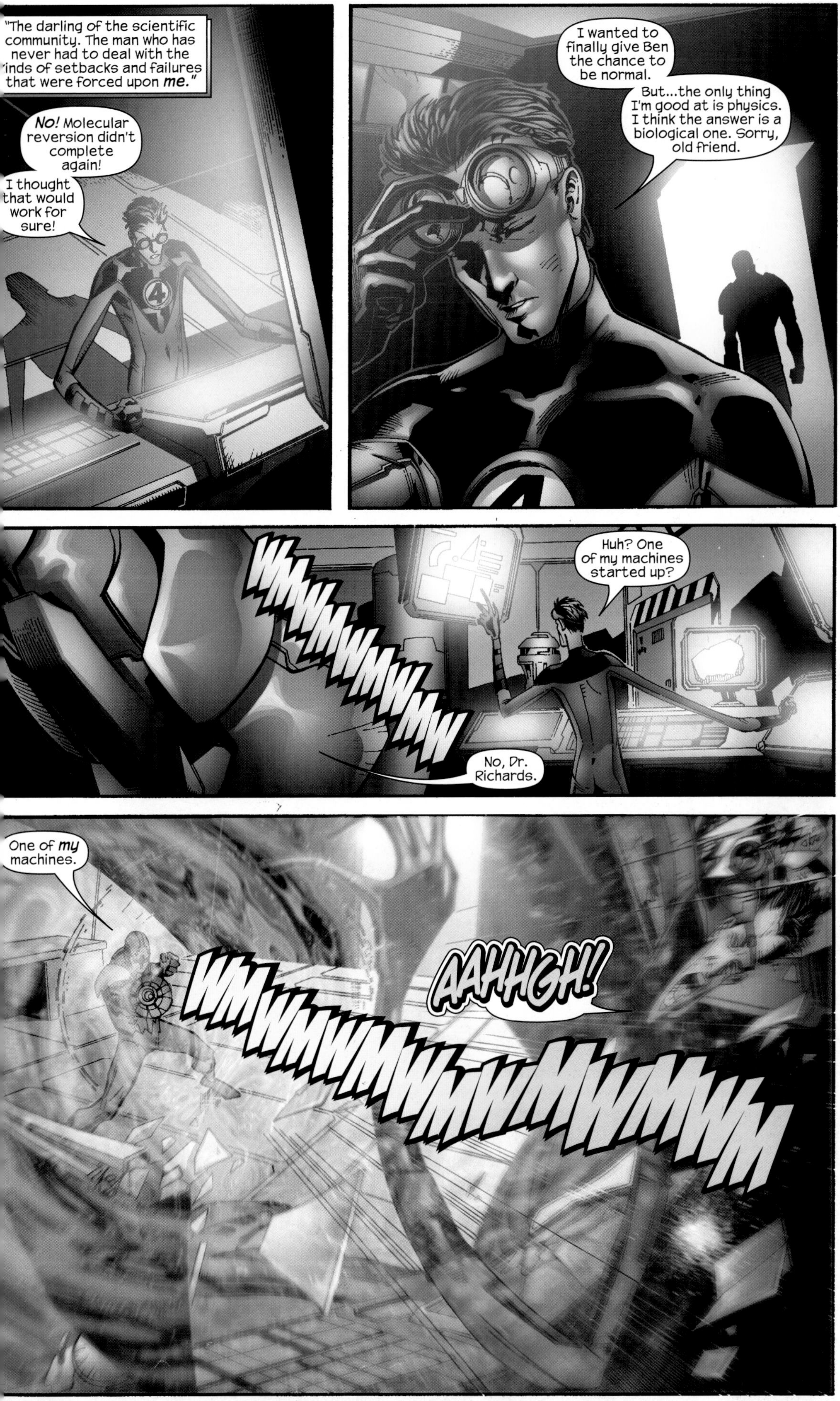
"The darling of the scientific community. The man who has never had to deal with the kinds of setbacks and failures that were forced upon *me.*"
No! Molecular reversion didn't complete again!
I thought that would work for sure!
I wanted to finally give Ben the chance to be normal.
But...the only thing I'm good at is physics. I think the answer is a biological one. Sorry, old friend.
WMWMWMWMWMW
Huh? One of my machines started up?
No, Dr. Richards.
One of *my* machines.
WMWMWMWMWMWMWMWMWM
AAHHGH!

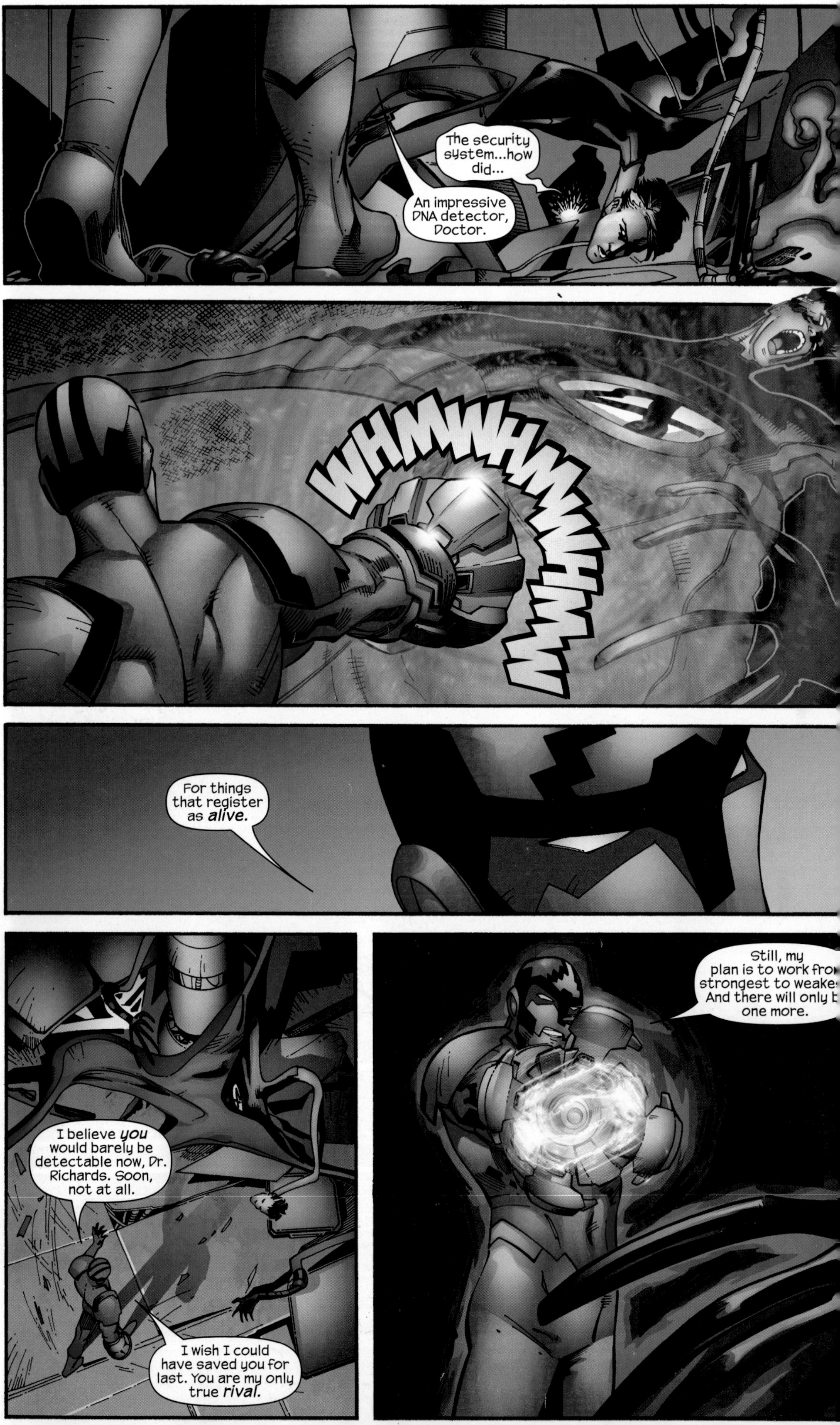

The security system...how did...
An impressive DNA detector, Doctor.
WHMWHMWHMWHMWHM
For things that register as *alive.*
I believe *you* would barely be detectable now, Dr. Richards. Soon, not at all.
I wish I could have saved you for last. You are my only true *rival.*
Still, my plan is to work fro strongest to weake And there will only b one more.

You'll...never...get...Susan...

You each have very distinct sonic signatures, Doctor.

It will take me no time to--

--find her?

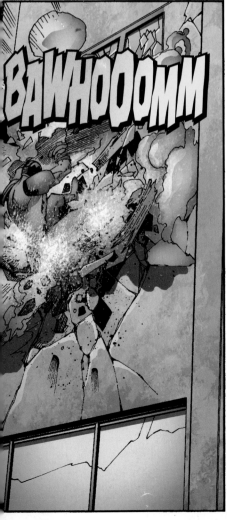

BAWHOOOMM

What was that about the weakest?

Guess I better break his fall with a force cushion.

...don't bother... ;coff;...

...his body is now a strange combination of matter and sound waves.

You don't have to worry about hurting him.

Oh really?!?

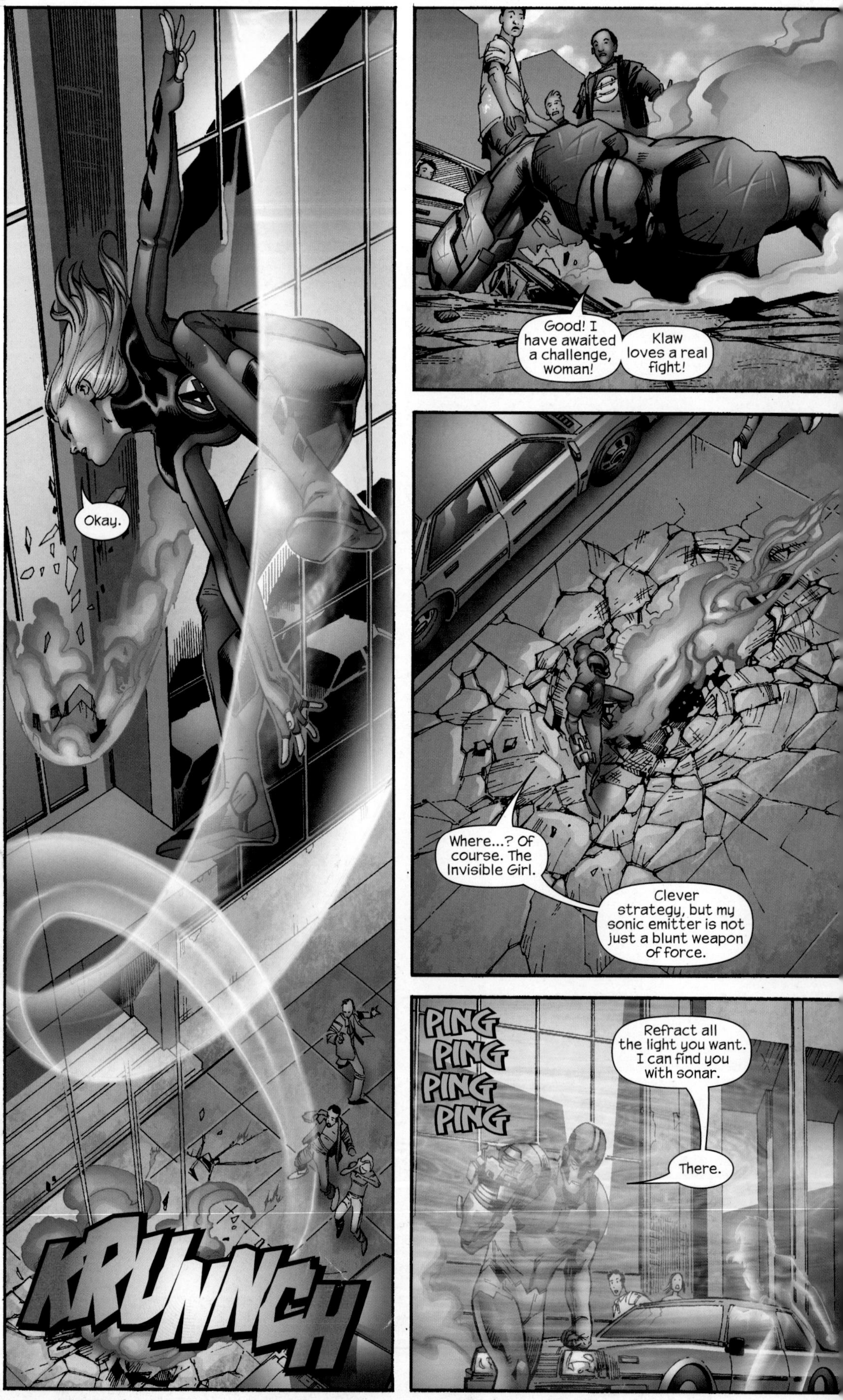
Okay.
KRUNNCH
Good! I have awaited a challenge, woman!
Klaw loves a real fight!
Where...? Of course. The Invisible Girl.
Clever strategy, but my sonic emitter is not just a blunt weapon of force.
PING PING PING PING
Refract all the light you want. I can find you with sonar.
There.

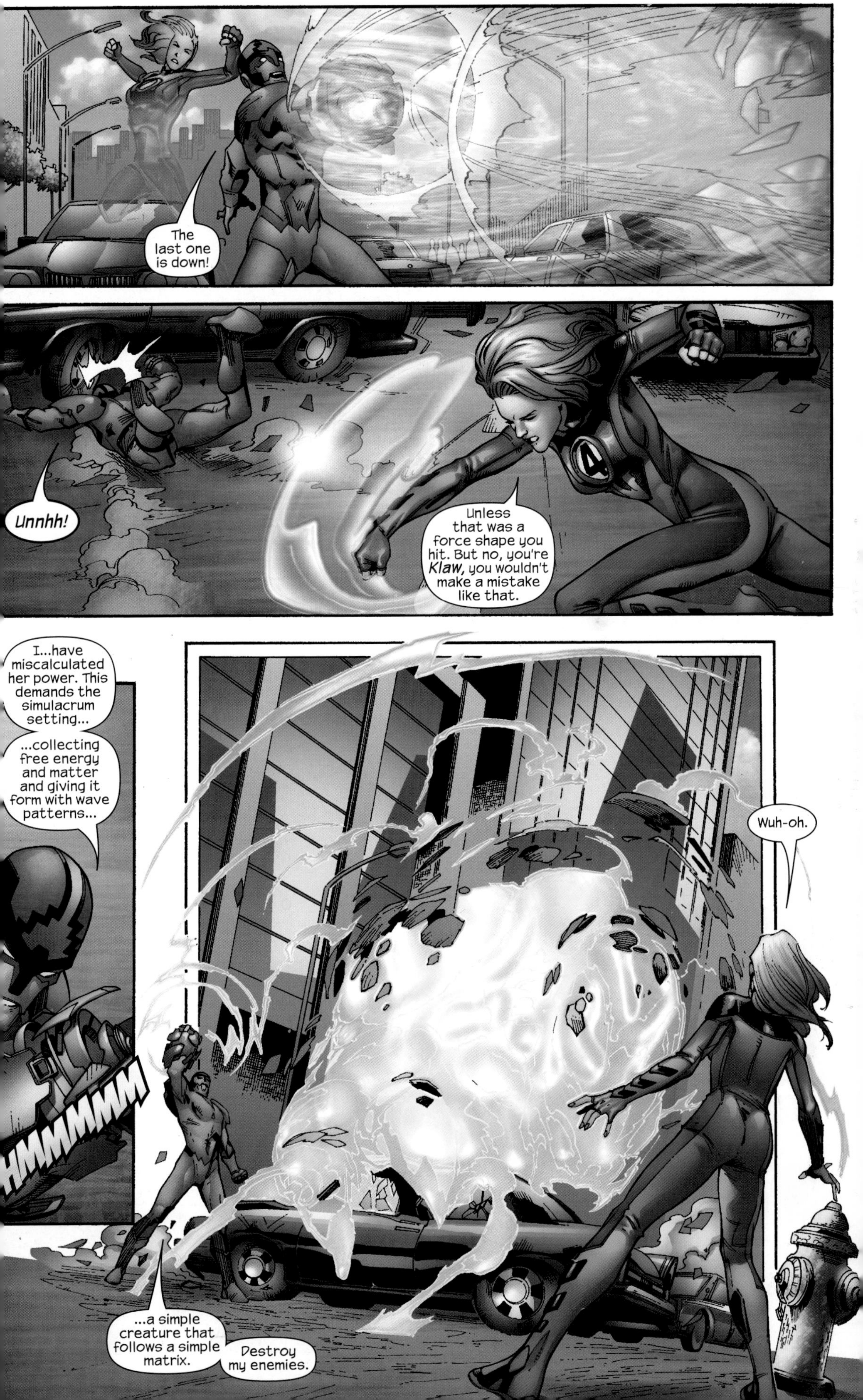
The last one is down!
Unnhh!
Unless that was a force shape you hit. But no, you're *Klaw,* you wouldn't make a mistake like that.
I...have miscalculated her power. This demands the simulacrum setting...
...collecting free energy and matter and giving it form with wave patterns...
HMMMMM
Wuh-oh.
...a simple creature that follows a simple matrix.
Destroy my enemies.

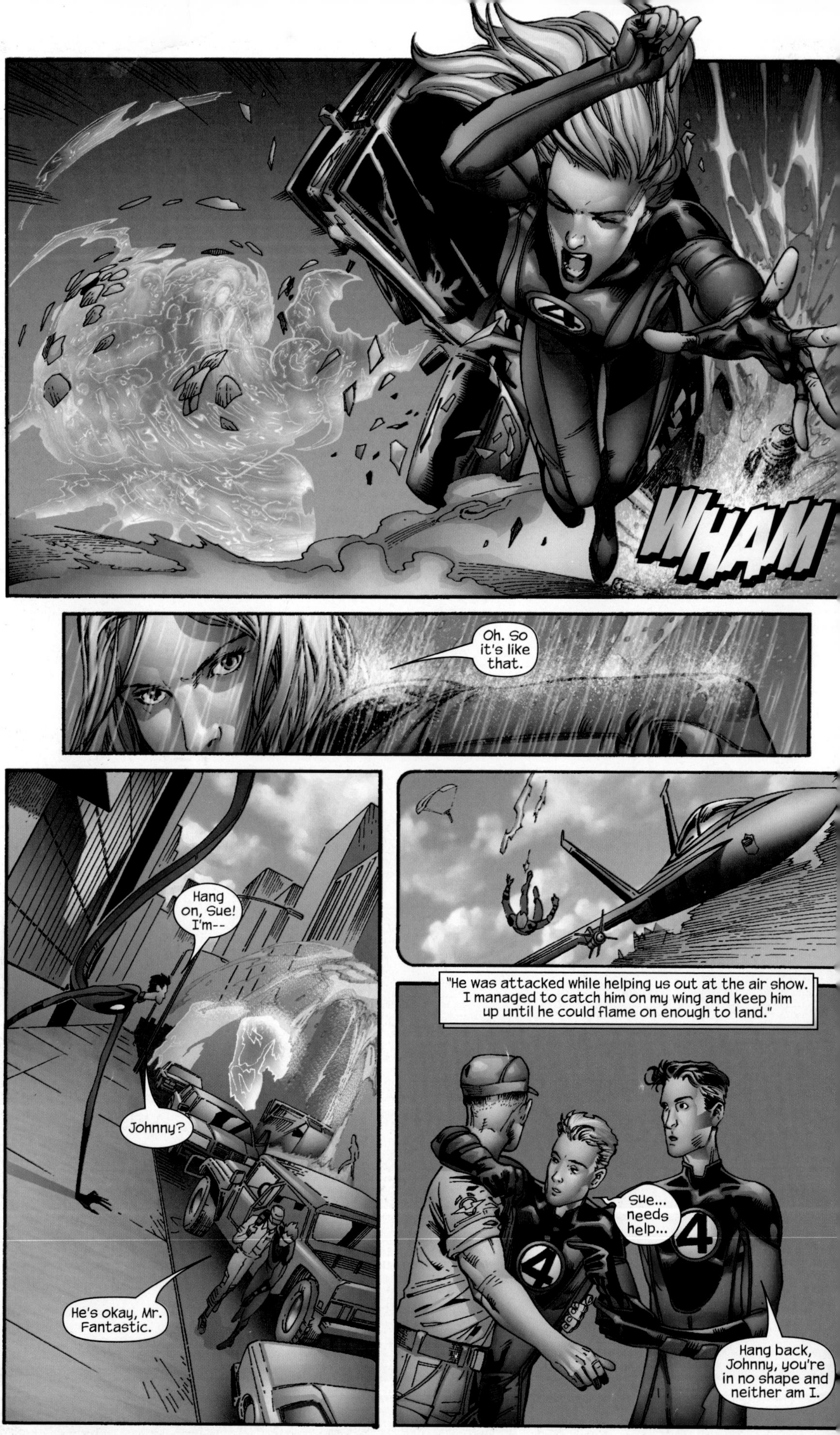
WHAM
Oh. So it's like that.
Hang on, Sue! I'm--
Johnny?
He's okay, Mr. Fantastic.
"He was attacked while helping us out at the air show. I managed to catch him on my wing and keep him up until he could flame on enough to land."
Sue... needs help...
Hang back, Johnny, you're in no shape and neither am I.

"Besides, I'm getting the idea..."

THUD

"...that Sue has this under control."

Oh, now that *rocks!* Go sis!

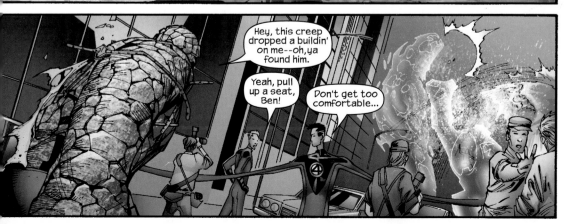

Hey, this creep dropped a buildin' on me--oh, ya found him.

Yeah, pull up a seat, Ben!

Don't get too comfortable...

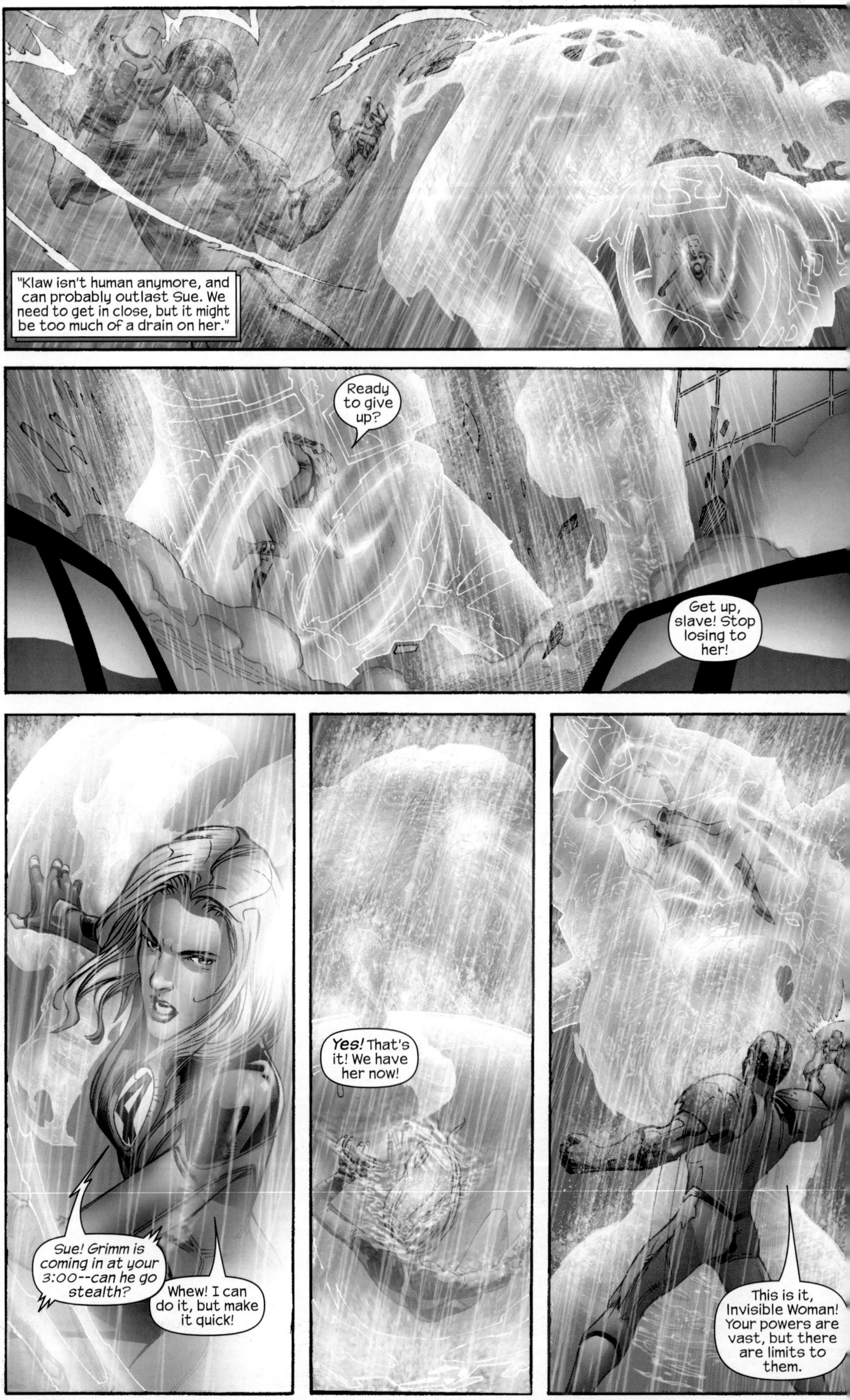
"Klaw isn't human anymore, and can probably outlast Sue. We need to get in close, but it might be too much of a drain on her."
Ready to give up?
Get up, slave! Stop losing to her!
Sue! Grimm is coming in at your 3:00--can he go stealth?
Whew! I can do it, but make it quick!
Yes! That's it! We have her now!
This is it, Invisible Woman! Your powers are vast, but there are limits to them.

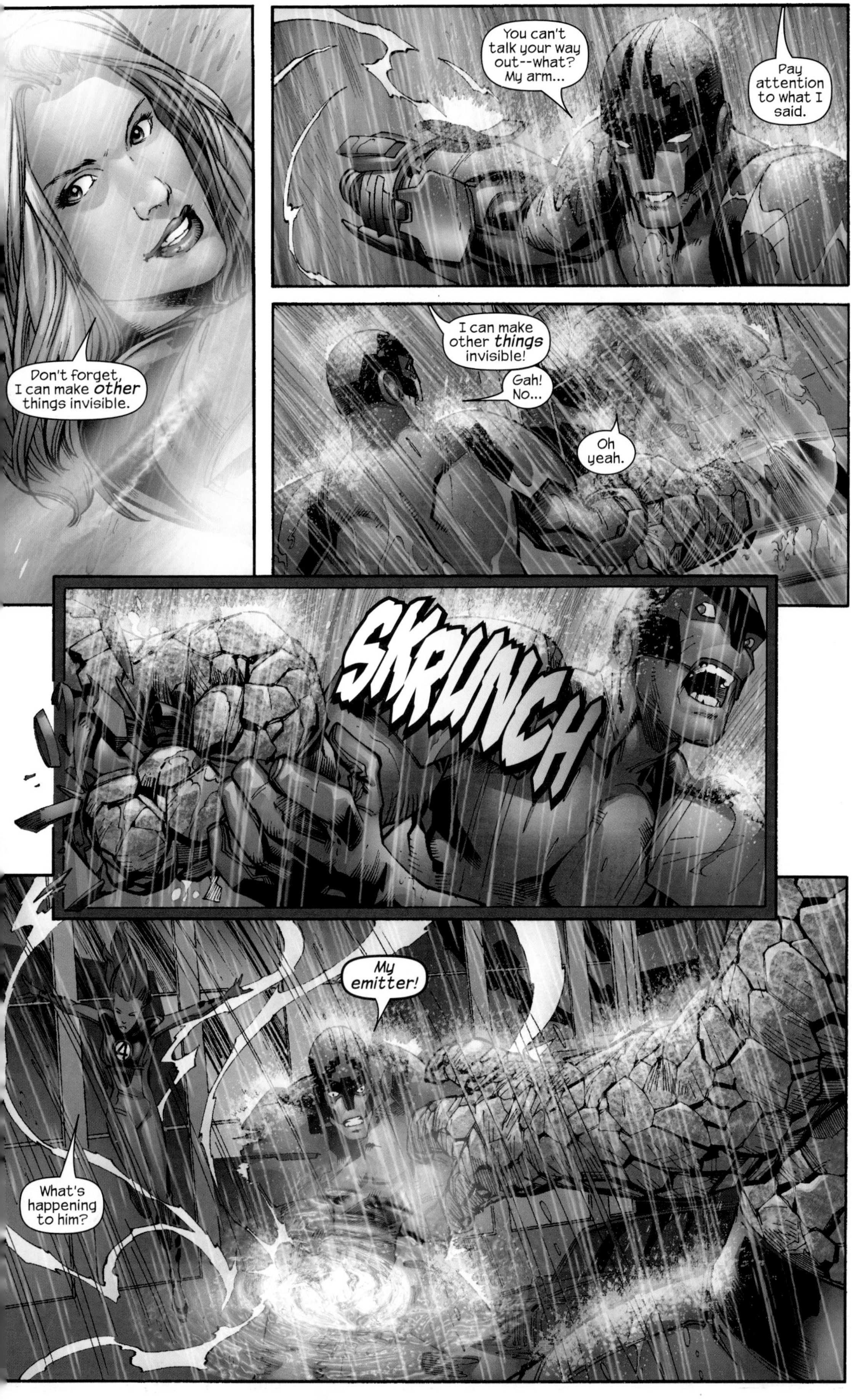
Don't forget, I can make *other* things invisible.
You can't talk your way out--what? My arm...
Pay attention to what I said.
I can make other *things* invisible!
Gah! No...
Oh yeah.
SKRUNCH
My emitter!
What's happening to him?

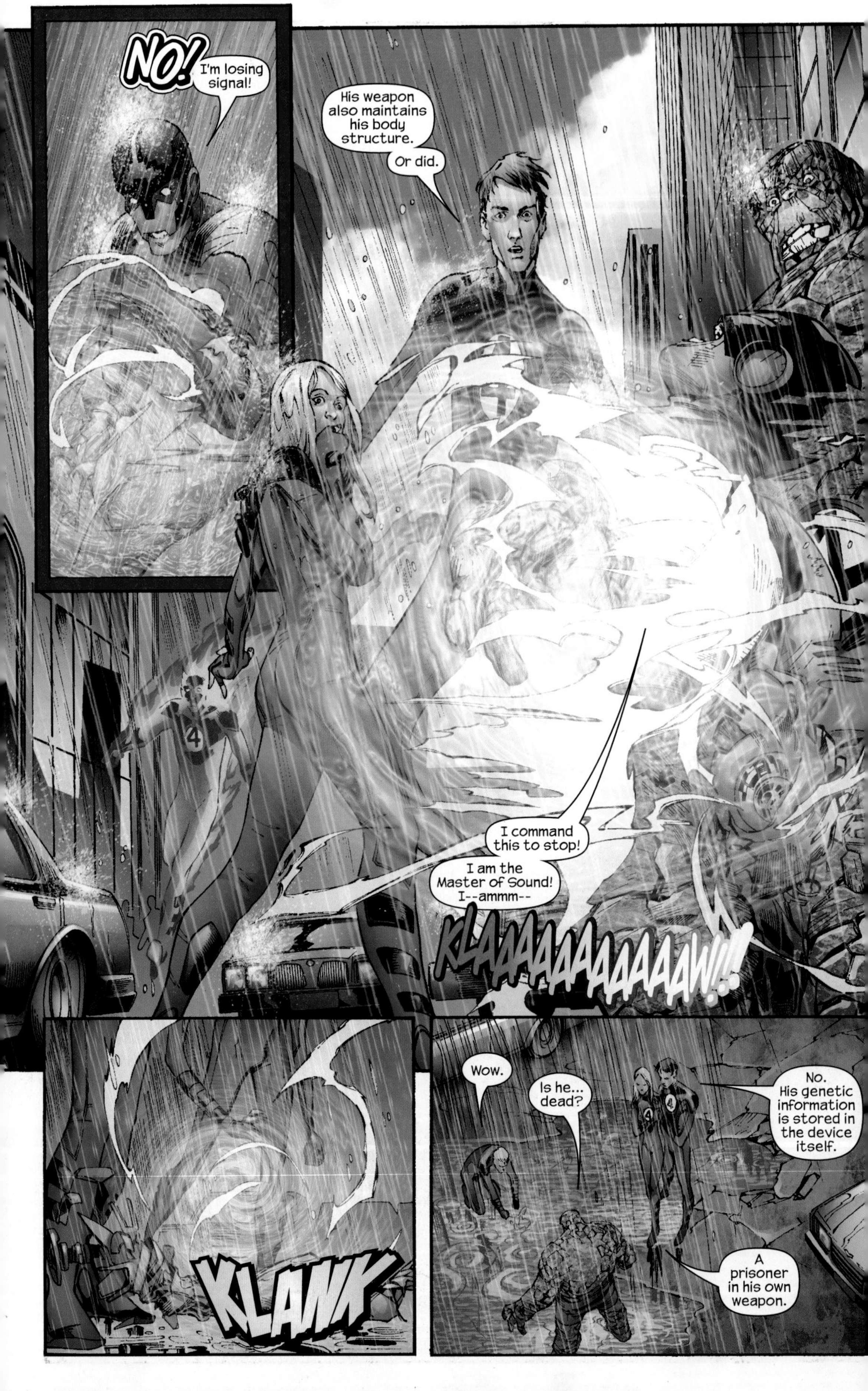

NO! I'm losing signal!
His weapon also maintains his body structure.
Or did.
I command this to stop!
I am the Master of Sound! I--ammm--
KLAAAAAAAAAAAAW!!!
KLANK
Wow.
Is he... dead?
No. His genetic information is stored in the device itself.
A prisoner in his own weapon.

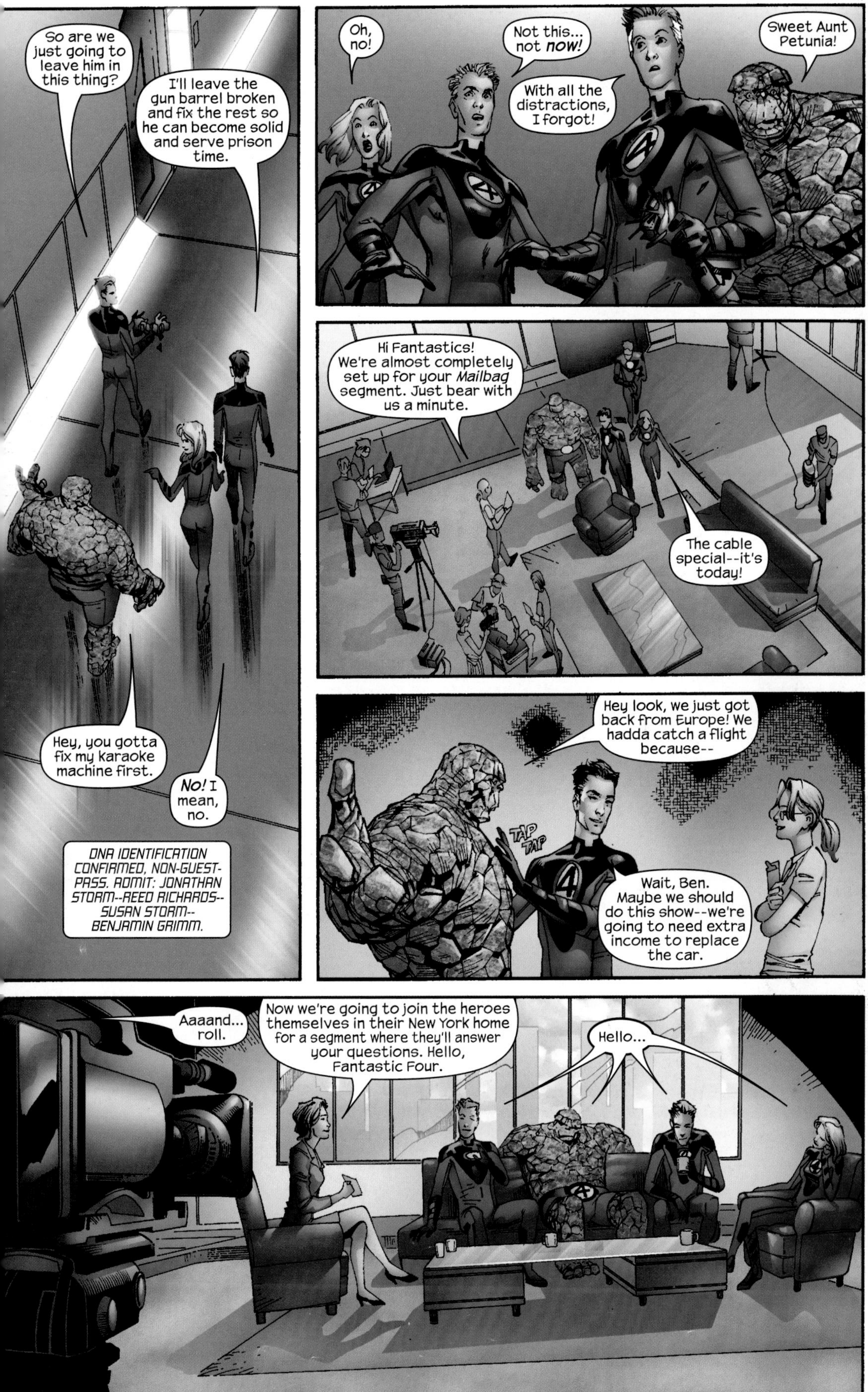
So are we just going to leave him in this thing?
I'll leave the gun barrel broken and fix the rest so he can become solid and serve prison time.
Hey, you gotta fix my karaoke machine first.
No! I mean, no.
DNA IDENTIFICATION CONFIRMED, NON-GUEST-PASS. ADMIT: JONATHAN STORM--REED RICHARDS--SUSAN STORM--BENJAMIN GRIMM.
Oh, no!
Not this... not NOW!
With all the distractions, I forgot!
Sweet Aunt Petunia!
Hi Fantastics! We're almost completely set up for your Mailbag segment. Just bear with us a minute.
The cable special--it's today!
Hey look, we just got back from Europe! We hadda catch a flight because--
TAP TAP
Wait, Ben. Maybe we should do this show--we're going to need extra income to replace the car.
Aaaand... roll.
Now we're going to join the heroes themselves in their New York home for a segment where they'll answer your questions. Hello, Fantastic Four.
Hello...

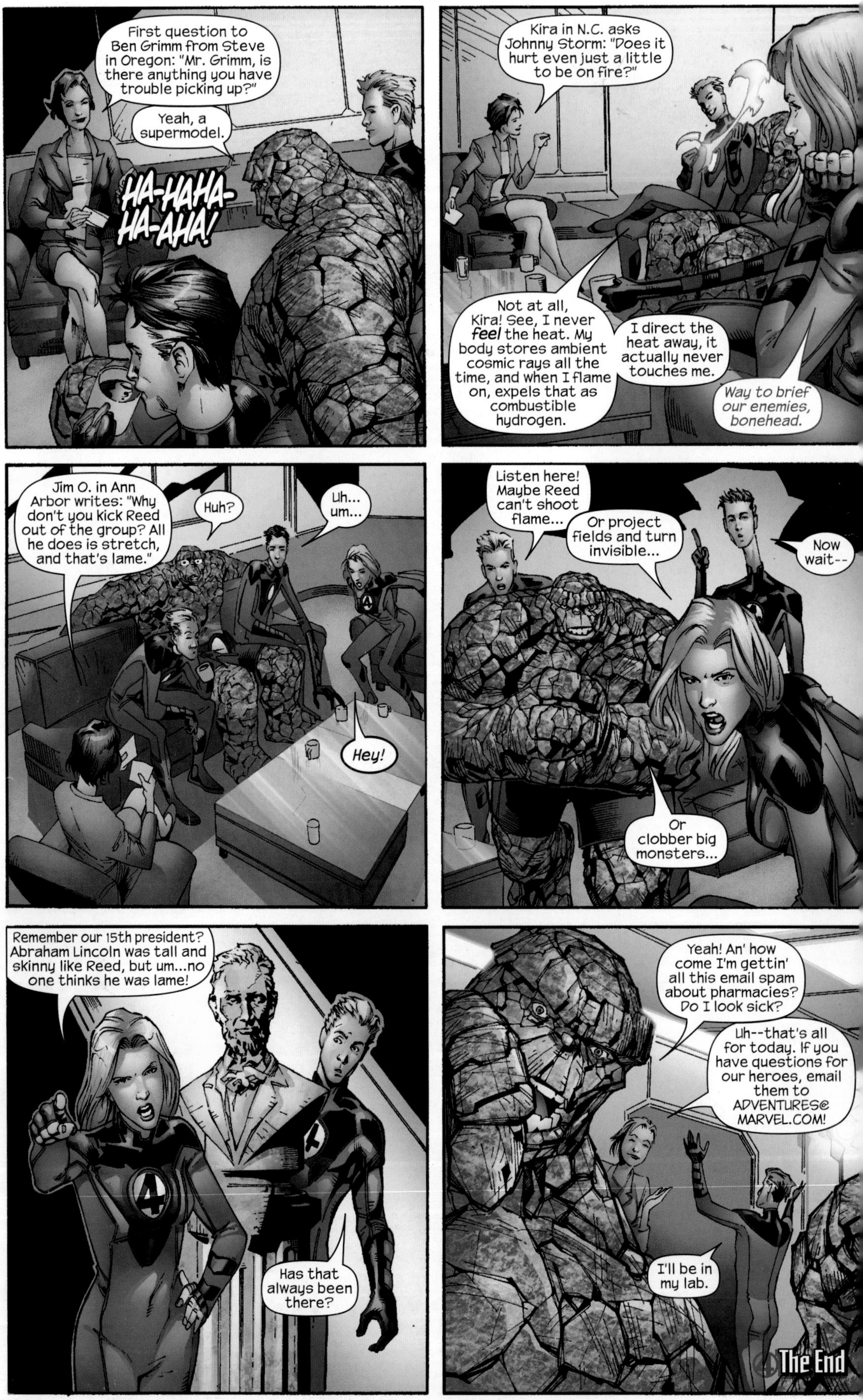

First question to Ben Grimm from Steve in Oregon: "Mr. Grimm, is there anything you have trouble picking up?"
Yeah, a supermodel.
HA-HAHA-HA-AHA!
Kira in N.C. asks Johnny Storm: "Does it hurt even just a little to be on fire?"
Not at all, Kira! See, I never *feel* the heat. My body stores ambient cosmic rays all the time, and when I flame on, expels that as combustible hydrogen.
I direct the heat away, it actually never touches me.
Way to brief our enemies, bonehead.
Jim O. in Ann Arbor writes: "Why don't you kick Reed out of the group? All he does is stretch, and that's lame."
Huh?
Uh... um...
Hey!
Listen here! Maybe Reed can't shoot flame...
Or project fields and turn invisible...
Now wait--
Or clobber big monsters...
Remember our 15th president? Abraham Lincoln was tall and skinny like Reed, but um...no one thinks he was lame!
Has that always been there?
Yeah! An' how come I'm gettin' all this email spam about pharmacies? Do I look sick?
Uh--that's all for today. If you have questions for our heroes, email them to ADVENTURES@MARVEL.COM!
I'll be in my lab.
The End